Lonesome Little Colt

Lonesome Little Colt

BY C.W. ANDERSON

COLLIER BOOKS

DIVISION OF MACMILLAN PUBLISHING CO., INC.

NEW YORK

COLLIER MACMILLAN PUBLISHERS

LONDON

Macmillan Publishing Co., Inc.
866 Third Avenue, New York, N.Y. 10022
Collier Macmillan Canada Ltd.

Library of Congress catalog card number: 61–12352
ISBN 0-02-041490-0
Lonesome Little Colt is published in a hardcover edition by
Macmillan Publishing Co., Inc.
Printed in the United States of America
First Collier Books Edition

5   6   7   8   9   10

To the Bedells and their ponies

On a farm in the country there were many, many ponies of all sizes and colors. They were all beautiful, with long flowing manes and tails. Each one had a little colt, and they all lived happily together.

Each little colt stayed close beside its mother. Bluebell was a gray pony. Her colt was red-gold, and she was very proud of him.

Calico's colt was bigger than the others, with long slim legs, and she was very proud of *him*.

Goldie had a lovely little colt of a light-gold color, and she was *very* proud of him.

When the flies were very thick, she always brushed them off her colt with her long silky tail. It made the colt very happy to know that his mother was always thinking of him.

But there was one little colt who had nobody to be proud of him. His mother had died, and he got his milk from a bottle each day.

He tried to stand close to Bluebell, but her colt kept him away. Bluebell was his mother, and he did not want any other colt near her.

One day he stood very close to Bluebell as she and Brownie rubbed each other's backs. He was very happy and felt almost as if he had two mothers. But the colts saw him and chased him away.

When the little colt tried to come near Calico, her colt saw him and kept him away.

Then the little colt thought that the dog, Spot, might be his friend. But Spot saw another dog and ran to join him.

The little colt felt very sad and
lonely. All the other colts had mothers and
he had nobody.

But two children on the farm had seen how lonesome the little colt was. Mary said to Tommy, "We must be very nice to that little colt that has no mother."

They petted the little colt and played with him. "What a nice little colt," they said. Now he was much happier.

Every day Tommy and Mary came
to see the little colt. As soon as he saw
them, he came running. Now he felt that
somebody really liked him.

When Tommy and Mary petted the little colt, the others came around too, but the lonesome little colt got the most petting.

But Tommy and Mary noticed that even the smallest colt would not let the little lonesome colt come near his mother.

"He misses his mother so," said Mary. "We must tell Daddy. Maybe he can think of something to do for that lonesome little colt."

A few days later the children saw their father drive into the yard. Then he opened the door of the trailer and led out a little pony. She was the color of gold and the most beautiful pony they had ever seen. "She lost her colt when it was born," he said. "Maybe she will like to be a mother to our lonesome little colt."

The little colt whinnied when he saw her and hurried over to her. The lovely pony whinnied back to him.

The beautiful pony nuzzled the little colt so softly when he stood beside her. Now there was no one to chase him away. He had a mother of his own.

The little colt stayed so close to his new mother's side that he was like her shadow. She was so beautiful and gentle that he was very proud of her. And he knew from her kind ways that she was proud of him. Now, at last, he belonged to somebody.

C. W. Anderson grew up in Wahoo, Nebraska, and studied at the Art Institute of Chicago. His first book, *Billy and Blaze,* was published by Macmillan in 1936. Since then, nearly a million Billy and Blaze Books have been sold, and Mr. Anderson has come to be recognized as America's foremost author-illustrator of horse stories. He has written such favorites as *The Blind Connemara, C. W. Anderson's Complete Book of Horses and Horsemanship, Blaze and the Forest Fire, Blaze and the Lost Quarry, Blaze Finds the Trail, Blaze and the Gray Spotted Pony,* and of course *Billy and Blaze*—all available in Collier Juvenile Paperback editions.